NOTHING IS INOPERABLE

BE_A_DEFEATER

THAKUR RUDRA PRATAP SINGH

ISBN 979-888591559-5

This book is dedicated to my Parents.

I got inspiration from them to write.

Contents

Foreword

The novel contains the life-story of a boy, who had hallucination problems. He had imagined a scientist, as his friend. In his childhood, the family and friends supported him and made him realise that the scientist was real and treated the imaginative character as their family member, along with the imaginative character the boy has invented a lot of things, a day the truth was revealed but the boy had a strong will he realised the truth and got to know about his capabilities.

Preface

ReferToForeword

Acknowledgements

A BIG THANKS TO ALL READERS, FAMILY, NOTION PRESS, SRIS FAMILY AND TEACHERS.

Prologue

Main characters.

BOY - Sameer

Scientist - Paresh

Mother and Father - Mr. Singh and Mrs. Singh

Friends - Prachi, Adi, Dimpy and Adam

ONE

Welcome Sameer To This World!

Today (21 July 1978) is a day of joy for Singh's as they have welcomed a new baby boy today, they named him Sameer. Sameer is a very healthy baby boy. Everyone in the family is very happy. All the family members are wishing Sameer a fruitful and healthy life.

Suddenly, the head doctor sprinted into the ward. She was really very frightened, she stated, "The baby suffers from 'Hallucination'." All the relatives seemed to be sad.

Someone asked, "What is Hallucination?" The doctor replied, "In this disease the sufferer imagines person, thing or other object which really don't exist. It is very dangerous and frightening too."

Mr. Singh (Sameer's Father) replied, "Sameer is just born, if we keep good care of him, he might be well by next year." The doctor agreed. Two days passed; Mrs. Singh was still unknown to her child's illness.

Finally, Sameer (along with his parents) was now back to home. His father took a left his job and took care of Sameer. (Without letting Mrs. Singh know about Sameer's illness). Sameer seemed to be well.

TWO

1ST BIRTHDAY

Today was 21 July (1979); It was Sameer's first birthday. His parents organised a wonderful event, they invited Pop-Star, everything was going nice.

Suddenly, they saw Sameer sitting in a corner. He was murmuring, "Hey! Kailash, you're a great scientist, I want to cut the cake along with you, You're my best friend."

Mr. Singh was shocked he explained his wife the whole case. They called up the doctor. Doctor examined him, "He is imagining Kailash, who doesn't exist as his best friend; I think we should start giving him medicines, this is an inoperable disease but then also we'll try our best."

The doctor prescribed the medicines and fixed weekly appointments for a year (In advance) with Sameer.

Mr. Singh tried to explain Sameer that Kailash doesn't exist it's just him imagination but the doctor warned him because Sameer could even get depressed or would suffer a heart attack, as he took Kailash' matter very seriously.

Mr. & Mrs. Singh treated as if Kailash was real, this made Sameer very glad that his parents had allowed Kailash to live along with him.

THREE

SAMEER- AN INVENTOR

Sameer (Along with Kailash) invented a car one day, which could run on O^2. The family and the medical practitioners were very shocked, also glad to know that Sameer himself has done such a great invention, but Sameer (Aged 5) was unknown of this, he dedicated his success to Kailash. His parents and the doctor never allowed him to go out and play with other children because if he could know the truth then it would be very dangerous.

Days passed; Sameer was very happy with Kailash. Mr. & Mrs. Singh were very much sorrow for their child. Always they tried to find a way to cure Sameer. They never left Sameer alone at home. Even they slept with Sameer (And the imaginative Kailash).

One day they took Sameer to the marketplace, Sameer liked a robot-elephant (cost $5), they bought a pair ($10) for Sameer and Kailash. Sameer went back to home and showed the elephant to Kailash, he liked it.

FOUR

Sameer Wants to Play Outdoor

Sameer woke up. It was a shiny day, Mrs. Singh called him for breakfast. He along with Kailash had nice breakfast.

He asked, “Maa, why I and Kailash don’t go out to play like other children in the locality.”

Mrs. Singh had nothing to answer, she allowed him to go outside from now onwards.

As, Sameer reached the play area, he saw four children (Prachi, Adi, Dimpy and Adam) playing Hopscotch.

As they saw Sameer Adi stated, “Let’s run away this boy sees the spirit of a scientist named Kailash (who doesn’t exist).”

All of them ran away.

Sameer with tears in his eyes ran back to home, he explained the whole event to his mother.

She replied, “Don’t cry my child; Kailash is like your brother he’s not a spirit, they are just saying non-sense.”

She told her husband about the same. They consulted the doctor. The doctor called up Prachi, Adi, Dimpy and Adam. He explained Sameer's case to the children and asked for their help. The children and their guardians agreed. They also treated Kailash as live and invited Sameer every day to play with them and treated Kailash and Sameer very kindly.

FIVE

SAMEER'S 10TH BIRTHDAY

Today is 21 July 1988. It's Sameer's birthday again, but 2nd celebration after Sameer's birth. In these 10 years his parents have struggled a lot, they have been guardians of Kailash (an imagination).

This year the doctor advised them to have a grand celebration of Sameer's birthday. They organised a local party and invited Sameer's friends and all the relatives. Sameer was very excited to cut the cake as this was the 1st time, he was cutting the cake. Everyone enjoyed a lot there was a DJ setup for all dance lovers.

Finally, the celebration was over and everyone was back home. As usual, Sameer took his medications and went to sleep with his parents and Kailash.

The next morning, Sameer suddenly woke up and cried out, "Where is Kailash? I have searched him everywhere even I've forgotten how he really looked."

Mr. & Mrs. Singh exclaimed, "The medicines are working."

They took Sameer to the clinic. The doctor examined him and concluded that he was better the reports have been improved, this is a big step of recovery when a patient is unable to recall the imaginative character.

The doctor said, “It is the perfect time to tell Sameer about the truth of Kailash.”

Sameer’s parents replied, “Will it be depressive for him?”

The doctor said, “Yes, it can be depressive but if we don’t reveal the truth now than Sameer would always be waiting for Kailash to return and the disease would grow.”

The doctor called Sameer in.

“Hey! Sameer, where is Kailash?”, The doctor asked Sameer

Sameer answered, “He is away from morning, even I am unable to recall him properly.”

“What if I tell you where he is?”, asked the doctor

“Yes, please tell I’m alone without him”, said Sameer

“He doesn’t exist”, replied the doctor

“How can you say that, he is like my brother”, he asked

“Sameer, my kid there is no Kailash in real; it was just your imagination because you hallucinate(imagine) things that do not exist in real this is a mental disorder, we acted that Kailash is real only to make you happy”, The doctor explained him

SIX

SAMEER DECIDES TO START A NEW LIFE

Sameer was crying loudly; he was very sad to know that Kailash do not exist. He thought to run away, but he had a strong will, it stopped him to do any wrong things and lead a sorrowful life.

He accepted the truth, but was very sorrow about his parents, he wanted to thank them because just to keep him happy his parents treated his imaginated friend as his relative.

Even they bought him a pair of everything one for himself and the other for Kailash. Then also he shouted at him when they talked something about existence of Kailash. He lived in the room upwards for a week alone, he didn't even allow anyone to enter the room.

Finally; a day Sameer woke up, unlocked the room went downwards to his parents and thanked them. He promised them to live a happy life from now with his family and would start a new life without any thoughts about Kailash.

SEVEN

Sameer Gets to Know About his Capabilities

Sameer's parents were confused about continuation of Sameer's studies as he had never gone to school before; then they remembered that how he invented the car that would run on O^2.

Sameer's mother asked, "Do you remember you have invented a car?"

Sameer exclaimed, "A car! How could I invent a car?"

His father told him and tried to make him remember about his invention.

Sameer finally recalled the formulae and set up a new invention.

All of his relatives encouraged him and appreciated his invented O^2 capable car.

This all inspired him and this time he tried to invent something that would make people younger. He had to travel all around the globe to gather all the natural and artificial ingredients for his experiment.

His family was financially strong, they travelled along with him and helped him collect all the chemicals and plant uproots.

He collected all the required materials and finally back to his home after 2 years. He went to his lab and started the experiment, he mixed all relevant things he worked 5 hours a day in his lab; several days passed Sameer's experiment was in trial stage, a Spanish named Carlo' Tofu (aged 85) volunteered. He gave him 5 drops of the solution, the person wrinkled, shrivelled, his hairs grew and he was now of 17.

His experiment was successful.

EIGHT

SAMEER GOT HONOUR

Sameer's experiment was successful and businessmen from US visited him to buy the formula. There was a quarrel between all businessmen; so, they decided to have an auction.

The auction started:

Someone shouted---

50000$

Followed by---

80000$

100000$

200000$

Finally, Charlie(UK) declared---

10million dollar

The formula was sold. It was the most expensive formula in the world, Sameer was honoured as World Record Holder and was also honoured by the Council and Union Ministers of the locality.

Everyone in the world praised Sameer, being ill he had such a wonderful capability. Sameer was an inspiration for all.

It was surprising that this great record is achieved by a 15-year-old boy. It was a proud moment for his country and the world.

NINE

SAMEER- APPOINTED AS A SCIENTIST

Sameer was appointed by th national space organization as an inventor and scientist for nuclear missions team head. He continued his profession. He was appointed at age of 19 when he had invented more than 100 of things. He married with a Brahmin girl. Singh family's generation was very fruitful and proud.

THE END

ThankYou

The Author

Notes

Notes

Report Errors

All errors or problems found may be reported to the author @ 8077438405.

About The Author

The author is born on 3June2009 in UttarPradesh. He studies in Stone Ridge International School, Rudrapur, Uttarakhand. He is the founder of NEA APP PUBLISHING CO. He devotes all his success to his parents (Deepti Chauhan-Mother) and (Peeyush Kumar- Father). He is also thankful to all his teachers, his grandparents and family.

ThakurRudraPratapSingh
(AUTHOR)

9 798885 915595

Printed by Libri Plureos GmbH in Hamburg, Germany